MAXIMILIAN P. MOUSE, TIME TRAVELER

YANKEE MOUSE

GETTYSBURG ADDRESS OBSERVER

magic wagon

BOOK 2

Philip M. Horender • Guy Wolek

visit us at www.abdopublishing.com

For my parents, who have been in the bleachers cheering since day one —PMH

Published by Magic Wagon, a division of the ABDO Group, PO Box 398166, Minneapolis, Minnesota 55439. Copyright © 2014 by Abdo Consulting Group, Inc. International copyrights reserved in all countries. All rights reserved. No part of this book may be reproduced in any form without written permission from the publisher.

Calico Chapter Books™ is a trademark and logo of Magic Wagon.

Printed in the United States of America, North Mankato, Minnesota.
052013
012014

 This book contains at least 10% recycled materials.

Text by Philip M. Horender
Illustrations by Guy Wolek
Edited by Stephanie Hedlund and Rochelle Baltzer
Cover and interior design by Neil Klinepier

Library of Congress Cataloging-in-Publication Data
Horender, Philip M.
 Yankee mouse : Gettysburg Address observer / by Philip M. Horender ; illustrated by Guy Wolek.
   p. cm. -- (Maximilian P. Mouse, time traveler ; bk. 2)
 Summary: Maximilian is still trying to use his borrowed time machine to get to a meeting between Farmer Tanner and a developer, but instead he finds himself watching President Abraham Lincoln deliver the Gettysburg Address in November 1863.
 ISBN 978-1-61641-958-5
1. Lincoln, Abraham, 1809-1865. Gettysburg address--Juvenile fiction. 2. Mice--Juvenile fiction. 3. Time travel--Juvenile fiction. 4. United States--History--Civil War, 1861-1865--Juvenile fiction. 5. Gettysburg (Pa.)--History--Juvenile fiction. [1. Lincoln, Abraham, 1809-1865. Gettysburg address--Fiction. 2. Mice--Fiction. 3. Animals--Fiction. 4. Time travel--Fiction. 5. Adventure and adventurers--Fiction. 6. United States--History--Civil War, 1861-1865--Fiction. 7. Gettysburg (Pa.)--History--Fiction.] I. Wolek, Guy, ill. II. Title.
 PZ7.H78087Yan 2013
 813.6--dc23   2012050546

TABLE OF CONTENTS

Chapter 1

GETTYSBURG

The time machine stood cooling in the corner. Its acorn shell exterior was covered in a layer of frost that was beginning to melt and pool on the floor.

Maximilian noticed a small window and made his way to it. As luck would have it, the fastener turned, the spring released, and it slowly swung open.

The air was cold, like it had been when he left Nathaniel's. He was becoming more and more hopeful that the time machine had worked and he was somewhere on the Tanner homestead.

Maximilian was on a mission to save his home in Tanner's Glen. When he learned that Farmer Tanner was being foreclosed on, he knew he had to do something as mouse of the house. He had met Nathaniel Chipmunk III and borrowed Nathaniel's time machine.

The time machine had taken Maximilian back in time to Boston in 1773. He had tried once more to get back to the glen. But, nothing looked familiar.

Maximilian spotted a nearby storm drain that would be a perfect ladder. He made his way to the dewy grass below.

It was becoming clear to Maximilian that he was in a much more **rural** setting than Boston. A noise on the opposite side of the house peaked his curiosity.

Maximilian moved around the side of the house. He discovered several carriages and wagons making their way past. A little drizzle was beginning to fall and storm clouds were gathering in the sky. Maximilian decided to follow the tide of people, being careful to remain out of sight.

He passed by several houses, taverns, and stores, many of which were decorated with red, white, and blue **buntings**. Ahead of him, in the distance, a dark plume of smoke billowed from a black locomotive pulling in to a train depot.

A familiar feeling was beginning to creep into Maximilian's mind—one of despair and hopelessness. The clothing on the people in the streets was different from those of Boston. But, they were not like the clothes Maximilian was used to seeing around Tanner's Glen.

A large crowd had gathered at the train station by the time Maximilian had arrived. The men, women, and children seemed abuzz. Many were trying desperately to get closer to the loading ramp. Maximilian tried to gain a better place by moving behind one of the turnpikes near the railroad tracks.

All at once, the crowd began clapping and cheering. Maximilian strained to see who was getting such a warm welcome. As he did so, a sign above the train depot caught his attention. It was a name, written in bold uppercase lettering . . .GETTYSBURG.

A tall, slender man emerged from the train. He was dressed simply in a black suit. Maximilian could not believe how tall he was! Even from twenty yards away, Maximilian

could see that the man towered over the **spectators**.

The man nodded to the crowd and placed a top hat on his head. The more Maximilian watched, the more captivated he became with this well-respected man.

A middle-aged man in a suit stepped to the forefront. He extended his hand to the train's passenger and dipped his head in **reverence**.

"Mr. President, on behalf of the citizens of Gettysburg, let me say welcome. We are truly honored that you were able to make it," the man said in a soft, steady voice.

"David, the events that **transpired** here over these past months have changed not only the course of the war, but the course of this country," the president replied.

Maximilian continued to study the crowd. The admiration they paid to their president astonished him. It was clear that this small, country town had witnessed something remarkable. The townspeople were looking to him for peace.

The president's group began to make its way slowly up the main street. In no time, Maximilian had made up his mind to follow.

As the crowd parted at the train platform, a shudder ran up Maximilian's spine. His eyes fixed on what had been hidden by the president—rows and rows of cedar coffins.

Maximilian cinched his **waistcoat** tighter as the rain steadied. In the distance, a crow called.

Chapter 2:
STOWAWAY

By now, it had been raining for several hours. Maximilian had all he could do to avoid the large puddles that had collected along the path.

Much to Maximilian's amazement, the president and his host were making their way back to the house that held the time machine. A bronze plaque hung outside the entrance of the home. It read *David Wills, Esq.*

Maximilian watched as the president removed his top hat and ducked through the narrow door frame. He met a petite woman wearing a powder-blue dress. She curtsied and motioned the president's aides in the direction of the top of the stairs. David Wills's wife, Catherine, had prepared her personal suite for the president.

Despite the rain, Maximilian could still see people gathered outside the Willses' home. They hoped to catch a glimpse of the president.

Maximilian followed the president to Catherine's quarters. Two men carefully placed the president's chest in the corner.

"Mr. Lincoln," one of the men said, "Mrs. Wills has prepared dinner downstairs in the parlor for you and a number of guests. Please join them at your earliest **convenience**."

The aide exited the room and closed the bedroom door behind him, leaving President Lincoln alone. Or so Lincoln thought. He didn't see the small, gray field mouse watching his every move.

President Abraham Lincoln removed his rain-soaked overcoat and hung it on the back of the door. Being a mouse, Maximilian was used to the large size of his surroundings. But, he continued to be amazed at just how tall President Lincoln was. Maximilian was curious as to how Lincoln would manage to sleep in Catherine's miniature bed.

Lincoln ran his hand over his face. He sat for a minute in a rocking chair next to the bed. Then, he opened a brown, leather bag to reveal a journal, inkwell, and pen.

The pen caught Maximilian's eye almost immediately. The body of the pen was finely crafted bone. Its tip was polished metal. Lincoln was careful to place the pen and the journal next to one of two lamps that had been lit in the bedroom.

Maximilian's stomach growled loudly. He was reminded of just how hungry he was. Since the time machine was safe in the attic, he decided to find food. Maximilian removed his drenched coat and vest and hung them over a nail in the side molding.

Darkness had fallen on the bedroom. As Lincoln stepped outside to join the others for dinner, Maximilian was close behind.

The Willses' house was warm and inviting. The staircase wound to the front entrance and to the adjoining parlor. Inside, thirty-seven guests were eagerly awaiting the president's arrival.

Maximilian was working hard to keep up with the president. All eyes turned to President Lincoln as he entered the dining room. It was the perfect cover for Maximilian to enter undetected.

Maximilian was amazed by the smells in the dining room. He detected sweet potatoes, roasted turkey, and steamed asparagus. He was certain there was more delicious food on the table.

The Willses' maid brought the dinner guests some warm, freshly made bread and a variety of jams. Just then, the proud host raised his glass and began making a toast.

"To the preservation of the **Union**. To the struggle for human freedom and equality. And to the men who gave the ultimate **sacrifice** that we may gather here this evening," David Wills said. "We honor your final resting place tomorrow on the fields of Pennsylvania."

Everyone at the table nodded in agreement and drank from their glasses. The toast was followed by the clink of utensils, several heated discussions, and an occasional **compliment** to the feast.

The house servants worked quickly to meet everyone's needs. In their haste, small chunks of food made their way to the floor and to Maximilian's waiting paws. Maximilian took his time enjoying the fine meal.

Every free moment he had, his mind found its way back to his family. He knew that if the time machine would work properly, his home would be saved and his loved ones would never know he had been gone at all.

Chapter 3:
DINNER WITH THE PRESIDENT

The evening was filled with **banter**, but had some very serious moments. Many of the serious conversations surrounded the next day's ceremonies.

"Absolutely splendid that you were able to make it to Gettysburg on such short notice," a round fellow said. "Your being here certainly helps with the healing process that we are confronted with."

Lincoln had stopped eating. He rested his chin in his hands with his elbows on the oak table.

"Well, after receiving my formal invitation and then the one that David penned to me personally, I had to attend," Lincoln said. "I had heard reports from General Meade. I felt

that sending a staff member on my behalf to speak at the cemetery's **dedication** would not be enough."

"The recovery process has been slow," David said. "I think slower than most thought it would take."

Maximilian was full. He picked up on the conversation just as David was explaining how the National Soldiers' Cemetery had been created.

Many of the men who died during the battle at Gettysburg had been buried in mass graves. Others had been kept in cool, damp cellars during the hot summer months. So, a special committee asked the governors of eighteen Northern states to collect money for a cemetery. Shortly after, workers began mapping out the new cemetery and reburying the dead.

Maximilian was surprised that such details were being discussed at a dinner.

"Much of the country really has no idea what we're still going through four months after the battle," Catherine chimed in, taking her husband's hand in hers. "In many ways, we're still fighting this battle."

"That's why when you accepted our invitation to the dedication, it meant so much to all of us," David said. "Have you given much thought to what you'll be saying at the service tomorrow?"

Maximilian waited along with everyone else at the dinner table for President Lincoln's response. Lincoln stared at his plate and thought for a moment.

"I find myself being constantly reminded just how far we've come as a nation," Lincoln finally began. "And of how much we've endured since we became a country eighty-seven years ago. As 1863 comes to an end, I wonder what lies in store for us in the upcoming years."

Maximilian did some quick math. His **detour** in Boston was in 1773. Now he sat in Gettysburg, Pennsylvania, ninety years later! Maximilian didn't know how to feel. Should he feel excited that the time machine had taken him closer to his goal? At this point, he needed any sort of hope.

Chapter 4:
A FRIGHTENING POSSIBILITY

Maximilian decided to rest quietly in the parlor. At eleven o'clock, the familiar chime of his pocket watch woke Maximilian. He struggled to remember where he was.

The lights had dimmed. Maximilian noticed the **silhouettes** of guards pacing in front of the Willses' home. It appeared the rain had stopped.

David Wills and President Lincoln sat alone in front of a crackling fire. Lincoln looked somewhat relaxed and comfortable.

"This really is quite an honor, Mr. President. We are very appreciative for your attendance tomorrow," David said.

"You've been a loyal supporter of mine, David," Lincoln responded. "My heart is heavy with all that has happened these last few years."

Maximilian moved closer to the brick **hearth**.

"How is the family doing in Washington?" Wills asked, changing the subject.

Lincoln drew a deep breath. "Things have been difficult, as you might have expected," he said, sweeping his hair away from his eyes. "Little Tad became quite ill before my departure. Mary was rather concerned with me leaving at such a time."

Wills nodded. "I can understand her worry," he said.

"I didn't see it fit to back out at the last moment," Lincoln said. "Although I'd be lying if I said my thoughts weren't at least partially elsewhere."

Maximilian decided it would be wise to check on the time machine. He needed to prepare a few things before trying a third trip. He made his way back up the stairs toward the president's room to get his coat. As he walked, he was aware of the possibility that he might never see his mother or his home again.

The door was open just enough for Maximilian to let himself into the bedroom. He gathered his belongings and scampered up the crown molding and through a small crack in the ceiling. In the attic, the time machine stood glistening in rays of moonlight.

Chapter 5:
SILENCE

O nce Maximilian knew everything was settled with the time machine, he sat down. He watched the time pass slowly on his pocket watch. He willed the minutes to go by faster.

The rain had stopped and the natural noises of a rural town had returned. Maximilian decided to explore Gettysburg a little. With all that he had seen and heard, he was interested in finding out more about this small town.

Maximilian scurried through the window and down the storm drain. He again found himself on the rain-soaked ground. He pulled his tail close to him and was thankful that he had dried his coat. Maximilian put his collar up and made his way toward the town square.

Maximilian glanced back at the Willses' estate. He could see President Lincoln pacing slowly in the bedroom window. Maximilian thought he must be forming his speech for the next day.

The road was wet beneath Maximilian's padded paws. Even though the rain had stopped, the clouds were thick. Maximilian didn't know exactly where he planned on going.

Gettysburg was surprisingly quiet. It was nothing like the busy Boston that Maximilian had just left. A horrible smell hung in the air. It caused him to hide his nose behind his wool collar.

Maximilian did not stray far from the Willses' home. He was careful to always keep it in sight. The town square was a circular patch of grass in the center with several streets branching in various directions. They were like the like spokes of a wagon wheel. Many of the homes and storefronts that Maximilian passed were dark.

Maximilian walked cautiously. He avoided the water that stood in the roads. The wind threw stray drops of rain Maximilian's way. Just when he was considering returning to the

Willses' home, a light and the faint sound of music caught his attention.

For the first time since he had arrived in Gettysburg, he smiled and quickened his pace.

As he approached the base of an old barn, Maximilian became somewhat **wary**. He wasn't sure what he might be getting himself into. He was a stranger in this town after all. Not everyone he met would be as nice as his friend Oliver from Boston had been.

Maximilian managed to calm his nerves. He turned a small, brass doorknob on a door that led underneath the barn. Maximilian took a shaky step into the dimly lit tavern. Almost immediately, the music and talking stopped.

Chapter 6:
MAKING NEW FRIENDS

Maximilian lowered the collar to his coat and closed the door behind him. A dozen or so mice had stopped what they were doing to look at the stranger. From behind a broken fence post bar, a large rat wearing an apron broke the silence.

"Well, don't just stand there, come on in!" he said. He motioned for the piano player to continue with his song. The piano came back to life and Maximilian breathed a sigh of relief. The rat motioned for Maximilian to take a seat on a cork stool in front of the bar.

"Now what on earth is a youngster like you doing in a place like this, at an hour like this, and in a town like Gettysburg?" the rat asked with a smile.

He stood perfectly straight with both paws on his hips. Maximilian took a seat on the cork.

"That's a long story, mister," Maximilian responded, managing a smile of his own. "I just arrived in Gettysburg this afternoon."

The rat wiped his paws on his apron and poured a thimble of hot tea. He placed it in front of Maximilian.

"Well, you must have your reasons for being here. This one's on the house," he said with a friendly wink.

Maximilian warmed his paws on the hot thimble and sniffed the sweet aroma of the tea. It was a welcome change from the unpleasant smell that seemed to haunt this town.

By this time, another mouse had moved next to Maximilian at the bar. This mouse's clothes were old and worn. His cowboy hat sat teetering on his head. Maximilian noticed that one of his ears was torn with a jagged scar. He flinched as this mouse moved even closer to him.

"Whereabouts you from, youngster?" the stranger asked.

Maximilian took a minute to sip his tea. "I'm from Tanner's Glen," he said quietly.

"What's that?" the mouse yelled back. Maximilian jumped.

"He said he was from a place called Tanner's Glen!" the rat said, raising his voice. "You'll have to excuse old Chester," he said to Maximilian. "He came to Gettysburg with Wainwright's Fifth Maine Artillery Battery. All of that time spent with Union cannons has taken its toll on poor Chester's hearing." Maximilian watched as Chester placed the tip of a gunpowder horn in his ear.

"Colonel Charles S. Wainwright is a great man," Chester said. "One's hearing is a small price to pay for years of service with such a man."

The rat held his hand out to Maximilian. "The name's Rattigan," the bartender said. "Moses Rattigan."

"I'm Maximilian P. Mouse," Maximilian said, shaking Moses's paw firmly.

"Well, Maximilian, I reckon Tanner's Glen is in . . .," Moses paused. "New York? It sounds Dutch to me."

Chester leaned closer with the ear horn and shook his head in disagreement. "No, no, no, Moses," he said confidently. "Tanner's Glen is definitely in Connecticut."

They both looked at Maximilian to help settle the argument.

"To be honest, I'm not quite sure where Tanner's Glen is exactly," Maximilian said, trading glances with both the mouse and the rat. "I've never been that far from the glen until recently."

"Well," Moses said, "Gettysburg is an interesting place to find yourself on a night like tonight."

"Where are you staying?" Chester asked loudly. He spoke as if Maximilian and Moses were the ones with difficulty hearing.

"Oh, I'm staying at the Willses' place," Maximilian said. He took another sip of his tea.

Once again, all of the mice in the bar stared at Maximilian.

"Really? You are staying at David and Catherine's place?" Moses asked in amazement.

"Have you seen him?" the mouse at the piano asked. His eyes were as large as coasters.

"Seen who?" Maximilian asked. He was becoming more aware that everyone in the tavern seemed to be hanging on his every word.

"Why President Abraham Lincoln, of course," the mouse replied.

"Actually, I had the pleasure of having dinner with him just tonight," Maximilian said. Suddenly, the tavern erupted with cheers.

Chapter 7:
CIVIL WAR

"A round of tea on the house!" Moses exclaimed.

The mice were on their paws, hugging one another and clinking their thimbles together. Maximilian's chest swelled with pride.

"What is he like?" Moses asked, pouring himself an iced tea. The piano was louder than ever as its performer moved from one ivory key to the next.

"He seems like a man who is struggling with a heavy **conscience**," Maximilian said. He had to raise his voice to be heard over the commotion.

Moses and Chester nodded. "He's always given us that impression," Moses said. "I think that's one of the reasons that so many people and animals in the Union admire him."

"What happened here, Moses?" Maximilian asked. "What happened in Gettysburg?"

Moses wiped his brow. "That is a very complicated question, my friend," he said. He settled on his own cork. "Very complicated indeed." He was much larger than Maximilian and as they sat across from one another, it became even more clear.

"I don't know exactly where Tanner's Glen is, but I'm sure it's been affected by the events of the country these past years," Moses continued. "That's why Chester and I tried to determine what state Tanner's Glen is located in. We were trying to figure out which side you were on."

"Side? What sides are there?" Maximilian asked.

Chester, who had been quiet, chimed in, "Sides? We're in the middle of a civil war, youngster! Brother against brother, mouse against mouse."

Surprisingly, Maximilian was familiar with the term *civil war*. Several years earlier, Tanner's Glen had been part of a civil war of sorts. Jacob W. Mouse, Maximilian's schoolteacher, had taught his students just how bad it was. It had threatened everyone living in the glen. Maximilian still remembered Mr. Mouse being fearful and uneasy when talking about the civil war.

"The two sides at war with one another are the Northern states and the Southern states of our fair country," Moses said. "And it's gotten really nasty."

"Really nasty!" Chester echoed like a pet parrot.

The noise in the place had returned to a normal level. Maximilian sensed that he was entering into a serious conversation.

"It's a sensitive topic, you understand," Moses continued. "Every mouse here tonight is a **veteran** of this war. Every one of them is different today because of it." Maximilian's eyes again scanned the mice in the tavern.

"Simon, the one playing the piano for us this evening, fought next to his uncle at the first battle of Manassas," Moses said. He continued going around the saloon.

"Joseph is the one closest to the door. He fought with Buford's first division here at Gettysburg, where he was born and raised. Angelo is playing cards with Leonard. They fought shoulder-to-shoulder with the renowned General Joseph Hooker at Antietam."

Moses lowered his gaze and shook his head.

"What happened?" Maximilian asked.

"It's just that we lost so many good friends over those three days in July," Chester said. "We're hearing reports from the mice working in the nurse units that almost 3,000 horses perished at Gettysburg alone."

Maximilian's face became flushed. He felt sick thinking about his horse friends that worked the fields on Tanner's farm.

This must have been some battle . . . and some war indeed.

Chapter 8:
MORE OF THE STORY

Moses continued talking about the Civil War. Soon, Maximilian felt as if he were actually living what Moses was describing.

For a few moments, Maximilian forgot all about the time machine and home. He was fully **enthralled** with the rat's tale. It was like being around a campfire telling stories during summer in the glen.

"The Southern states are those below what humans refer to as the Mason-Dixon Line," Moses continued. "Maryland, Virginia, and every state south sided with one another. In fact, they went so far as to break away from our country entirely. They formed what they saw as their own **confederation**!"

"They broke away from the country!" Maximilian exclaimed. "Could they do that?"

His mind returned to Boston in 1773. He thought of Oliver's dream of fair taxes and representation for the colonies. To think that at some point in history, the colonies had successfully achieved their goal of self-rule only to divide later. This failure would have crushed his dear friend.

"Whether or not they could **secede** from the Union didn't matter. They did," Moses said.

Despite the passion Moses used to tell his story, Chester was beginning to doze at the bar. Maximilian's watch chimed midnight.

"That's it, Chester. It's midnight," Moses said. He placed his paw on his friend's shoulder.

Chester nodded groggily and made his way to the door. Angelo and Leonard had ended their card game and were close behind him.

"Look here, Chester," Angelo said in a thick Italian accent, "let me get that door for you. Lenny and I will be happy to walk you home."

Moses gave them a friendly wave and he and Maximilian watched them go.

"Where were we?" Moses began again. "Oh, right, the Southern states started their own country. Truth is, this division within our government had been going on for some time."

Simon stopped his playing and stretched his paws. He took his jacket from the standing coat rack and waved good-bye to Moses. He left the saloon with an exhausted yawn. Maximilian also noticed that Everett had left at some point without saying good-bye.

"Most mice you ask will say that the North and South disagreed over 'state's rights,'" Moses said. "But it really came down to the issue of slavery."

Maximilian's eyebrows rose with astonishment. He certainly had not expected Moses to say that.

"You seem shocked," Moses said, noticing Maximilian's surprise.

"I didn't realize that slavery existed in the United States," Maximilian replied. To him it seemed unbelievable.

"Why yes, my young friend. It had for many **generations**," Moses said, straightening himself on his seat. "Fact is, the Southern economy is dependent on it. Many Southern states mostly rely on farming crops, such as cotton and tobacco, for their livelihood."

"Like Farmer Tanner," Maximilian said. "Although he doesn't grow cotton or tobacco. He mostly grows corn and hay."

"Those are common crops here in the North. That is another reason I think that you may not be too far from Tanner's Glen after all," said Moses. "Cotton and tobacco are especially tough crops to grow. The South has relied on slave labor for a long time now."

"So, the South felt they should have the right to keep slaves to help on their farms? But, the North felt that slavery was wrong?" Maximilian asked. He was still trying to understand how Oliver's country of freedom and choice could allow one person to be enslaved by another.

"Well, I guess you could say the North didn't agree with slavery," Moses said, standing to stretch his legs and wipe down the bar. "The

North's economy is based mainly on industry, you know. So they didn't need slaves the same way the South did."

A flash of light tore through the tavern. It was followed immediately by thunder. Both Maximilian and Moses jumped.

"Well, looks like you won't be going anywhere anytime soon, youngster," Moses said. The sound of drops hitting the barn grew.

Maximilian looked at Joseph. Joseph was slumped in his seat with his hat pulled over his eyes, sound asleep.

"Can I fix you something to eat, Maximilian?" Moses asked.

"If it's not too much trouble," Maximilian said. He realized how long it had been since dinner and began to feel hunger pains.

Despite the renewed rain, the bar remained warm and dry. Moses fed the woodstove several new cedar chips. Then, he prepared a platter of nuts and seeds for Maximilian and him to share.

"So, the issue of slavery was what led to the South breaking away from the Union,"

Maximilian said. He removed the shell of a pale green pistachio.

"Well," Moses began, "like I said, it's complicated. Other factors were at work, but slavery played a big role."

A second blinding flash of lightning startled Maximilian. He continued to be amazed at how soundly Joseph slept at his table.

"It was soon after President Lincoln took office that the Southern states broke away," Moses explained.

"And Lincoln felt that the Union should stay together?" Maximilian asked between bites of nuts.

Moses took a swig of tea. "I believe that Lincoln thought that the federal government had every right to end slavery in the United States. I also think that Lincoln saw the individual states as having more in common than they did differences."

"Gettysburg must have been an important turning point in the war," Maximilian said, "if Lincoln thought it was important enough to come here from Washington."

Maximilian looked at Moses.

Moses nodded and said, "We're certainly hopeful, Maximilian. This war has gone on far too long already."

Maximilian and Moses finished their nuts in silence, listening to the rain fall steadily outside.

Chapter 9:
A SURPRISE IN THE NIGHT

Maximilian's watch chimed a single note. "That's quite the pocket watch," Moses said. "It's very handsome."

"It was a gift from my father on my first birthday," Maximilian said proudly.

"Well, he must have thought quite highly of you to give you such a fine gift," Moses replied.

Maximilian thought for a moment about what Moses had said and smiled.

"It's getting late, Moses, and I really should be getting back to the Willses' place," Maximilian said. He jumped to his feet and buttoned his coat.

They both looked outside at the storm.

"You're sure you'll be alright getting back safely?" Moses asked.

"It's not too far," Maximilian said after a slight pause. "Thank you, Moses. It was really nice speaking with you."

"Maximilian, you gave the old mice of this tavern a nice **distraction** from these past few months," Moses said in a **solemn** voice.

"We come here every night to listen to music, play cards, and share a few hours together. These past few years have really taken their toll on everyone—mice and rats included."

"I hope everything works out for this town," Maximilian said, moving toward the door.

"Be careful," Moses warned. "I'm not quite sure what you're used to in Tanner's Glen. But there are some mighty bad individuals about at night in Gettysburg."

Maximilian thought about waiting until morning to return to the Willses' attic. But he wanted to make sure that everything was okay with the time machine.

"I can't imagine too many people or animals are out in this weather," Maximilian said. He gave one last wave to the bartender as he backed into the night.

The rain was not as heavy as the previous day. But, the combination of clouds and lightning made for a rather frightening walk.

The shadows played tricks on Maximilian. The wind whistled through the trees. Every house looked the same. Every building that he passed seemed identical to the last. Before long, it became quite clear that he was hopelessly lost.

A voice whispered over the storm, "Maximilian." It was an **eerie** and unnerving voice.

"Hello?" Maximilian called out. He was careful not to bring too much attention to himself.

He continued walking. Once again, the voice called from over his shoulder, "Maximilian."

Maximilian stopped. He heard the autumn wind blowing through the slots of the shudders hanging from an old brick store.

Almost immediately after finding the source of the noise, Maximilian began to feel better. If there was one lesson he had learned from his experience these last two days, it was to trust his instincts. He felt that he was becoming more confident in himself every step he took toward finding his way back to the glen.

Maximilian continued walking at a steady pace. He began to look around feverishly for the town square and something he recognized. It was shortly after one o'clock in the morning when he heard his name called again.

This time it wasn't the wind and it wasn't the shudders. It was a large, calico cat standing under a dead thistle bush not ten yards away from him.

Chapter 10:
DISBELIEF

Maximilian froze in his tracks. He thought about running, but he knew outrunning a cat would be nearly impossible.

"Oh, please don't be afraid," the cat said in a **sinister** voice. "I did not mean to startle you. Where are my manners, Maximilian?"

The cat took a step forward. Maximilian could see that he was swinging a key on a long string. Maximilian's attention was drawn away from the key. It focused on the razor-sharp claw at the end of the paw.

Maximilian couldn't help but think of the night Nathaniel saved his life back in the glen. The owl had swooped toward him outside of Nathaniel's den. He shook his head of the thought and stood. He carefully watched every move the cat made.

"I am terribly disappointed to see you out this late at night," the cat said. It shook its head and made a *thst, thst* sound.

Maximilian was unable to move. He was rooted to the ground in fear. His eyes darted around searching for any escape route that he could find.

"How . . . how do you know my name?" Maximilian managed to stutter. The fur over his eyes was matted with sweat. He imagined that by now, the cat could sense how absolutely terrified he was.

"Why, I feel like I know everything there is to know about Maximilian P. Mouse," the cat said. It took a step closer to Maximilian. "You see, my small friend, I happen to live in the barn where you just spent your evening."

Maximilian's heart was pounding. He thought for sure the cat could hear that as well.

The cat stopped swinging its key and licked its lips cruelly. Maximilian had forgotten about the rain, lightning, and thunder. His entire focus was on the cat and managing to survive the next thirty seconds.

Maximilian had no other choice. In a split-second decision, he began running as fast as he possibly could. Pumping his arms hard, his legs strained through the mud. He couldn't afford to look back to see how close the cat was, but he could hear its heavy breathing. He imagined it closing fast.

Maximilian used his quickness, dodging around different things. He tried to make it as difficult as possible for the cat to make a move on him.

A sound was getting louder. Suddenly, Maximilian knew exactly what he heard—it was a locomotive. A train was coming!

Maximilian fought through the cramps that pained his legs. He desperately wanted to make it to the railroad tracks that were only feet away.

"Oh, Maximilian, it doesn't look good, does it?" the cat said from behind him. The question was followed by an evil laugh. Maximilian was astonished at how close the cat was.

By the time Maximilian reached the tracks, the train was bearing down on him. A decision had to be made.

Maximilian held his breath and jumped the first rail line. He felt for a moment that he would make it.

He **lunged** once more to make it across the second rail line, but his coat wouldn't let him. Maximilian's sleeve was stuck underneath a tie. He looked at the mighty train steaming toward him. Then, he glanced at the cat sitting on the other side, its tail waving back and forth.

The cat had begun to swing its key in circles around its finger again.

"I've decided to wait," he said with a sneer. "That train is going entirely too fast for me to cross. Good-bye, Maximilian."

Maximilian closed his eyes.

Chapter 11:
CLOSE CALL

Suddenly, a strong paw grabbed Maximilian by the collar of his coat. It dragged him to the opposite side of the tracks. Maximilian heard a tear and felt his paw come free. Just as the train barreled by him, he fell nose first into the mud.

Maximilian sat up and wiped mud from his eyes. It had happened so fast, he had no idea how he had managed to survive.

Squinting into the glow of the late autumn moon, he saw Moses's grin.

"Let's get you home," Moses said, helping Maximilian to his feet. "We have to be quick. This is a rail line from Harrisburg and won't be too terribly long. Once it passes by, we'll have your cat friend to deal with again."

Maximilian knew Moses was right. He dusted himself off. He felt frantically for his pocket watch. He was relieved to find it still sat securely in the bottom of his coat pocket.

Together Moses and Maximilian scampered along the railroad tracks. They used the tall wall of grass as protection as they went.

When the train eventually passed, they looked back. The cat sat looking at the tracks in shock.

"Come quickly," Moses instructed. "It's a straight shot to the Willses' home from here, but we have no time to waste."

Before Maximilian knew it, Moses had him standing at the base of the brick town house.

"Moses, I don't know what to say," Maximilian said, still breathing heavy. "You saved my life."

Moses wiped the sweat from his ears and peered down at him. "Maximilian," he said, "I've certainly come to appreciate friends, even more so than I did before the war. I consider you a friend. Please be careful in your travels. Good luck finding your way back to your beloved Tanner's Glen."

Maximilian hurried up the storm drain. He stopped to look back at Moses, but the rat was already gone.

Maximilian sat quietly. He had been foolish to venture out into a foreign place at night. He wouldn't always have a rat like Moses or a mouse like Oliver to be there for him. He had to be smarter.

Now Maximilian was safely back in the Willses' loft. He was startled by the hustling of feet up the staircase. Suddenly, a frantic knocking was heard on Abraham Lincoln's bedroom door.

It was shortly after one thirty in the morning on November 19, 1863.

Chapter 12:
WITNESSING HISTORY

The knocking had given Lincoln's guard the surprise of his life.

Lincoln was shaken by the **urgency** of the messenger. He was dressed only in a simple nightshirt when he opened the bedroom door. From Maximilian's perch, he could see that their conversation was calmer than he had thought it would be.

After several minutes, the messenger excused himself and left.

"That telegram was from home," President Lincoln explained to the confused guard. "My little boy was very sick, but he is getting better," he announced. He was unable to contain his relief.

Maximilian also felt relieved and very moved. He had known President Lincoln for less than a day. But, he felt a strong connection to him. The stories that he had heard and the strength that Lincoln displayed gave Maximilian the impression that he was a remarkable human.

Lincoln sat at the desk in front of the window with his face in his hands. Maximilian noticed his hair was thinning and beginning to gray. His face was wrinkled. Maximilian imagined the war had been hard on him personally.

Lincoln took his quill pen and dipped it carefully in his inkwell. He began to write. He finally looked as though his attention could now be devoted to the speech that he came to Gettysburg to deliver.

Lincoln wrote well into the morning. He stopped only to dip his pen in ink. The candlelight cast a golden hue on his long, thin fingers.

Fourscore and seven years ago our fathers brought forth on this continent a new nation, conceived in liberty, and dedicated to the proposition that all men are created equal.

Maximilian listened carefully as Lincoln read it aloud to himself.

Now we are engaged in a great civil war, testing whether that nation, or any nation so conceived and so dedicated, can long endure. We are met on a great battlefield of that war.
We have come to dedicate a portion of that field as a final resting place for those who here gave their lives that that nation might live. It is altogether fitting and proper that we should do this.

Maximilian sat quietly, his tail wrapped in a tight hug around his body. He enjoyed watching Lincoln. It amazed him how easily the words were coming to him now that he had received the good news regarding his son's health.

But, in a larger sense, we cannot dedicate—we cannot **consecrate**—*we cannot hallow – this ground. The brave men, living and dead, who struggled here, have consecrated it far above our poor power to add or detract.*

What would Moses and his fellow veterans say if they were here to see Lincoln writing his speech? Would they agree with his words, with his reflection on the war? Maximilian felt confident that they would.

The world will little note nor long remember what we say here, but it can never forget what they did here. It is for us, the living, rather, to be dedicated here to the unfinished work, which they who fought here have thus far so nobly advanced.

President Lincoln paused periodically to return his pen to the inkwell and to rest his tired eyes. The candle on his desk burned low.

It is rather for us to be here dedicated to the great task remaining before us— that from these honored dead we take increased devotion to that cause for which they gave the last full measure of devotion; that we here highly resolve that these dead shall not have died in vain; that this nation, under God, shall have a new birth of freedom; and that government of the people, by the people, for the people, shall not perish from the earth.

Maximilian imagined how proud Oliver would be to hear those words included in this speech. He watched Lincoln remove his glasses and place his pen on the desk.

Chapter 13:
MAXIMILIAN'S JOURNAL

It was very late, or very early, depending on how one looked at it. Either way, Maximilian had found that he was losing track of time altogether.

Just like in Boston, he was in awe of what he had witnessed in a short time. He was actually nervous for President Lincoln. And, truth be told, he was somewhat excited that he would hear the president's important speech.

Maximilian made his way back to the time machine. He peered inside the portal. He noticed his knapsack propped behind the driver's seat. He had nearly forgotten that he had brought several things from home!

Maximilian climbed inside the time machine and took stock of his belongings. But really, he was looking for one item.

Finally, he found it. Next to his compass and **canteen** was a small, leather-bound journal. He had kept a diary for one week as a school assignment last summer. He enjoyed putting his emotions on paper to reread later.

Maximilian ran his paw over the familiar binding. He opened the book to a blank page.

He dated the page November 19, 1863, and began writing.

Maximilian poured his thoughts and adventures onto the bare pages. He wrote about Nathaniel and his workshop. He added a section about Oliver, the Sons of Liberty, and dressing like an Indian to participate in the Boston Tea Party.

Next, he wrote about President Abraham Lincoln. He included Moses's tavern of Civil War veterans. Finally, he wrote about what lay ahead of him and of how tomorrow offered new hopes and new challenges. He only paused when his pencil lead needed to be sharpened.

It had been a long day—an eventful day.

He placed a ribbon bookmark after his entry and closed the journal. Maximilian put it back in his knapsack. Then, he folded his jacket and laid it on the floor next to the time machine. He rested his heavy head on his jacket.

Tomorrow was indeed an important day.

Chapter 14:
CURIOSITY

Dawn welcomed a bright and sun-soaked morning. The *tap, tap, tap* of an old redheaded woodpecker woke Maximilian.

Maximilian stretched his paws. Then, he groomed the soft fur on his tail and straightened his whiskers. He missed many things from home, but his soft, hay-stuffed mattress was near the top of the list.

Maybe tonight I'll be home, he thought.

As he was going through his morning routine, he could hear movement in the room below. Peering through the hole in the molding, Maximilian could see President Lincoln sitting at the desk.

Lincoln carefully folded the pearl white paper twice and slid it into an envelope. He rose and placed the envelope into the breast pocket of his coat. Then he hung the coat on the back of the bedroom door.

A moment later, the same door swung open. Lincoln's aide told him that breakfast had been prepared. The president paused to place his glasses on the nightstand before going downstairs.

Maximilian's curiosity tugged at him. He finally decided to take a quick look around. Using the molding, he carefully climbed down onto the president's bed.

He moved next to the luggage chest. This time it was bright enough in the bedroom for Maximilian to take a look inside at its contents. Even though President Lincoln was one of the most important figures in the world, his belongings were relatively basic.

Books, several photos, and clothing lay in the chest. Maximilian immediately recognized the president in the simple black and white pictures. He guessed that the other people posing with him must be family.

Without warning, the bedroom door slowly began to open. Maximilian's pulse raced, his eyes darting through Lincoln's belongings in search of a safe place. His gaze fell on the door and on Lincoln, whose slow stride led him back into his guest room.

Maximilian panicked. His right paw slipped from the lip of the wooden trunk. He flailed helplessly. He made one last desperate attempt to grab one of the buckles. But it did not work.

He was falling!

Chapter 15:
FREE-FALL

Maximilian continued to free-fall. It seemed as though he had been falling for minutes. He landed with a thud. But amazingly, he was all right! A black top hat had cushioned his fall.

Maximilian took a second to collect himself. Then, he quickly got to his feet. He was still in danger of being discovered. Maximilian was inside President Lincoln's top hat!

Looking up, Maximilian could see Lincoln at the door. The president was placing the glasses from the nightstand in the pocket that contained his speech.

Maximilian began throwing his weight against the side of the hat, trying to tip it over. He was a mouse caught in a trap.

Suddenly, Maximilian felt a sense of weightlessness beneath him. He fell forward, catching himself with his tail. It was such a strange sensation, it took him a moment to realize that the hat had been picked up. He was now being carried.

Being a gentleman, Lincoln had refused to put his hat on inside. Luckily, that bought Maximilian several more precious minutes. Hiding in the shadows of the hat, he decided to wait for the right opportunity to escape.

Lincoln jostled Maximilian as he walked downstairs. From the number of voices, Maximilian could tell a large group had gathered to see Lincoln off.

"Glorious day, Mr. President!" said David Wills.

"Glorious indeed, David," President Lincoln replied. "Your **hospitality** and support are greatly appreciated and will not be soon forgotten. You are an admirable man and would make a splendid public servant."

Maximilian could not see David's response to such a compliment. Instead, his view was of the sky and several wispy, early morning clouds.

Maximilian held his breath as the sun beat down on him. It was so hot and sunny out that the president would surely want to wear his hat.

"You will lead the processional to Cemetery Hill, Mr. President," another voice instructed. "Your horse is ready for you."

Maximilian prepared himself to jump, to run, to take advantage of any opening at freedom.

"It's too nice of a day to wear my hat, Jonathan. I trust you to carry it for me," Lincoln said. He handed the hat to one of his trusted aides.

As the brim tipped, Maximilian scampered away unnoticed. He ran out of the hat, down the aide's arm, and onto the back of the president's saddle.

Chapter 16:
THE RIDE

The **procession** began sharply at ten o'clock in the morning. It moved toward Cemetery Hill at the northern end of Cemetery Ridge. This was where the Army of the Potomac had halted the Confederate advance on the first day of battle.

Maximilian couldn't help but notice that the beautiful mare the president rode was too short for his long legs. Many of those who followed whispered amongst themselves at his feet narrowly missing the ground.

The group moved slowly toward the northern portion of town on its way to the battlefield. Along the way, the scenery changed **drastically**.

Maximilian felt like he was now seeing an entirely different village. One constant remained, however. The hideous odor seemed to get worse as they went. Then Maximilian's eyes fell on one of the most horrific sights he had ever seen.

Outside of town, Maximilian saw the ghastly skeletal remains of horses amongst the trees. Flies swarmed on the remains. Maximilian willed himself to look away.

"Not much farther now, Mr. President," a burly man said. Maximilian had been so distracted, he had failed to see Ward Hill Lamon ride next to the president. Lamon was the president's friend and self-appointed bodyguard.

Lamon had arrived earlier that morning. Most of his face was hidden behind a beard, although Maximilian noticed he had gentle eyes. Lamon wore a sash around his broad shoulders and a top hat similar to President Lincoln's.

He motioned the president in a new direction. Lincoln pulled his reins slightly west along the town's boundary.

Maximilian noticed that several townspeople had laid out tables with "souvenirs" from the battle. There were bullets, bayonets, buttons, officer badges, army-issued **canteens**, shell fragments, army caps, bloodstained rags, and even cannonballs.

At the base of Cemetery Ridge, a general with dark, sunken eyes and full sideburns, leaned over in his saddle. He pointed something out to the president.

Maximilian looked as well and saw a line of cannons and wooden makeshift fences. The landscape was peaceful. If Maximilian hadn't heard for himself of the dreadful events that had happened here, he would have thought of these cornfields and lush wheat fields as any other farmland.

"Think, Mr. President," the officer said with a slight Pennsylvania accent, "of the men who held these heights."

Lincoln sat quietly for a moment and closed his eyes to ponder this thought.

"Yes," he replied, "but think of the men who stormed these heights."

As war continued to rage and the fate of the country hung in the balance, President Lincoln's thoughts lay both with the Union and with the Confederacy. Lincoln refused to choose between friend and foe. He realized that they were one and the same.

Finally, they arrived at their destination.

Chapter 17:
SENATOR EVERETT

Lincoln dismounted from his horse. Maximilian decided to stay with the president. He still had several hours before he could start up the time machine.

Hurrying down the horse's beautiful, long tail, Maximilian scurried along undetected. He kept up with the president until he took his seat. A sea of **spectators** lay out before them.

Maximilian made sure to keep alert. One misstep and he could very easily be crushed or stepped on. Luckily, those at the ceremony were so captivated with President Lincoln, they failed to notice the small, gray field mouse accompanying him.

Maximilian scanned the crowd. Many there were dressed in Union military uniforms.

Others wore business suits and dresses. With the sun continuing to shine on the crowd, many of the women had opened parasols for shade. Others were waving fans to provide some relief from the early morning heat.

Maximilian saw movement out of the corner of his eye. Amongst several flower arrangements and wreaths sat Moses with the mice from the tavern. Maximilian was happy they were there.

The master of ceremonies, who happened to be Ward Hill Lamon, welcomed everyone. Next, Edward Everett, a senator from the state of Massachusetts, spoke. US flags flapped proudly in the breeze. They provided an appropriate backdrop for the speaker.

Maximilian settled on the cool grass. President Lincoln, despite being surrounded by security and friends, kept to himself. He appeared to listen closely to what Senator Everett had to say. Maximilian found himself paying more attention to Lincoln than he was to the speaker.

Senator Everett's speech went on for more than two hours. Maximilian wiped sweat from his brow and picked at a blade of grass to help pass the time. He noticed that Moses was speaking with Leonard and that Chester had fallen asleep.

Between 15,000 and 20,000 people had crowded around the speakers' platform. After a while, many wandered away to tour the battlefield. The crowd was getting smaller.

David Wills leaned in and spoke quietly to President Lincoln. "If they're leaving to tour the battlefield, they should know that unexploded shells have been **detonated** daily for the last week or so. They're taking their lives in their own hands."

No sooner had Wills finished this sentence, than Senator Everett ended his speech.

Lamon stepped forward and announced, "The President of the United States!"

Chapter 18:
THE GETTYSBURG ADDRESS

Lincoln removed his papers from his pocket and rose. Carefully placing his gold-rimmed glasses on the bridge of his nose, he unfolded his speech and drew in a deep breath.

Lincoln's Gettysburg Address consisted of ten sentences totaling 271 words. It was a sharp contrast to Senator Everett's two-hour speech.

Maximilian moved to the front of Lincoln's chair so that he could see and hear. Many who had left during Senator Everett's talk had hurriedly returned. Moses stood and Chester was awake with his ear horn pointed in Lincoln's direction.

President Abraham Lincoln delivered his speech with minimal emotion. With his simple words, he went beyond what had been said in the **Emancipation Proclamation**. Lincoln called for a **rededication** to the values outlined in the Declaration of Independence.

Maximilian could hear the words of both Oliver and Moses echoed now. In 1863, as in 1773, the belief in equality and opportunity for all was still a worthy enough cause to die for. Those who lay in the graves at Gettysburg and throughout the United States had not died in vain. They had died upholding the noble values that the country had been founded upon.

Maximilian could not have been prouder. That's why he was astounded and amazed by the reaction of the crowd.

Lincoln folded his papers and returned to his seat. Maximilian wanted to tug on his slacks and assure him that he had done a masterful job.

Maximilian noticed that the photographer who had set up his camera had failed to take a single shot because the speech had happened so quickly. It was only slightly longer than two minutes. Instead the shutter lay silent and the chance to capture history missed.

The audience was still. No one cheered. In fact, no one said a word. Maximilian could best describe their reaction as shocked, confused, and maybe even disappointed.

Even his friends from the tavern seemed underwhelmed. They were talking heatedly amongst themselves.

After a few minutes, Maximilian began to hear comments like "Is that all?" and "Did he finish?" ripple through the confused crowd.

President Lincoln himself seemed unfazed. Wills patted him on the back and Lamon commented in Lincoln's direction that the speech had been "touching." Maximilian agreed with them.

A round of rifle shots and a single cannon fire marked the end of the dedication. The crowd broke up and arrangements were made for a return trip to Washington.

Maximilian's attention returned to the time machine, to Tanner's Glen, and to getting back to saving his home.

Chapter 19:
BLESS YOU

Maximilian didn't know it, but the Gettysburg Address would be **debated** for years. Many thought the speech was dull, dishwatery, silly, flat, and even vulgar. Other journalists defended it as being a masterpiece of literature.

President Abraham Lincoln himself underestimated the weight of the words he had delivered. It was not forgotten over time. In fact, it defined how Lincoln was remembered as president.

President Lincoln decided to walk back to the Willses' home. So Maximilian walked as well. They were both tired, their thoughts elsewhere.

The time was nearing for Maximilian to put his faith in Nathaniel's time machine again.

They arrived back at the house shortly after three o'clock in the afternoon.

The guard stationed at the front of the house stood with perfect posture. He welcomed the president.

Lincoln's response was much more personal. "Any word on Tad?" he asked.

"No, sir. We can try by telegraph before you board," the guard responded.

"That's quite alright," Lincoln said. "I'll organize my things and be down shortly."

Maximilian followed Lincoln upstairs. He ran up the now familiar molding back into the attic. He had one more thing to do before he set the coordinates to the time machine.

Maximilian quickly unwrapped his journal from his knapsack and sharpened the dulled pencil. He wanted to capture everything that had happened while it was still fresh in his mind.

The scent of lavender and daisies floated across Maximilian's nose. Before he could catch himself, he sneezed. Even Maximilian was taken aback by how loud it had been.

President Lincoln finished latching his trunk. He paused for a moment and arched his gaze toward the hole in the molding where Maximilian sat.

"Bless you," the president said quietly. "Bless you, my friend." And he slowly walked out of the room.

Chapter 20:
THE GOLD BUTTON

Maximilian placed a period at the end of his last sentence. Then, he placed his red ribbon bookmark to mark the page and put the journal in his knapsack. Tomorrow he would be back home remembering this amazing trip.

Maximilian surrendered to one final temptation. He looked at the guest room where Lincoln had penned his Gettysburg Address. He stared through the hole in the ceiling molding. The room lay quiet and undisturbed. Nothing at all was out of place.

Just before Maximilian turned to go back to the time machine, something caught his eye. He climbed down the molding and onto the floor. An object lay at the foot of the bed.

Maximilian finally reached the mystery item and was amazed. A shiny, gold button lay on the floor! Maximilian held it in his paw and analyzed the eagle crest on the front. In one of the eagle's talons was an olive leaf sprig and in the other were three arrows. Maximilian had seen the exact same crest on one of the latches to Lincoln's trunk.

Maximilian had found one of the buttons to President Lincoln's coat. It was the perfect **memento** for his time in Gettysburg. And it was small enough that it would fit in the time machine. Maximilian held tight to the button and returned to the attic.

The time machine battery was showing almost 100 percent capacity. It was time.

2013, October, 15, Tanner's Glen.

The coordinates glared back at him, lit boldly in the darkness of the time machine portal. Maximilian knew the routine by heart now. His paw reached toward the start button. Taking a deep breath, he pushed it.

The time machine started to spin. Soon, the spinning was overwhelming. Then, it stopped.

Maximilian took a minute to collect his thoughts. After carefully unlocking the straps of the chair, he reached for the portal latch with his handkerchief.

Before he could undo the catch, a violent jolt threw Maximilian back into his seat. He tried again and was able to unlock the exit. A stiff waft of dust and dirt slapped Maximilian in the face. The rocking and shaking made it difficult for him to climb from the time machine.

At first, Maximilian's senses were on overload with noises and smells. His soft padded paws were on dirt-stained wooden planks. The high-pitched sound of scraping metal was deafening to his sensitive ears.

The room rocked and Maximilian braced himself on the wall. He coughed as the dirt made its way down his throat despite the handkerchief at his mouth.

Maximilian noticed that some glassware nearby had been wrapped in pages of an old newspaper. Maximilian squinted in an effort to make out the text. He unfolded several wrinkles in the paper. When he could read the words, he saw the paper was the *St. Louis Post-Dispatch*. The date was February 23, 1869.

Maximilian's heart sank. He continued to read. The disappointment he had experienced before was nothing compared to the shock and despair that replaced it.

"President Ulysses S. Grant anticipates that the completion of the country's first cross-continental rail line will ultimately usher in a new era of economic prosperity and help mend a wound that still cripples the United States since the . . ."

Maximilian felt faint. He sat on the wooden floor and tried to **comprehend** what he had just read. The words did not come easy.

". . . **assassination** of President Abraham Lincoln almost four years earlier."

About the Gettysburg Address

In 1863, the United States had suffered two long, trying years of civil war. In July, a small, rural town in Pennsylvania was the site of three days of fighting. Those three days helped change the tide of the war. They would prove to be a turning point in our nation's history.

The Battle of Gettysburg resulted in some 51,000 deaths. It would be forever etched in the history books with names such as Little Round Top, Devil's Den, the Peach Orchard, and Pickett's Charge.

Many of the wounded and dead were left in Gettysburg. They were kept in public buildings, private residences, and pastures that had served as makeshift hospitals. The citizens of Gettysburg worked together to create a national cemetery in the town.

President Abraham Lincoln was committed to preserving the Union and reunifying the country. He traveled to Gettysburg in November 1863 to help dedicate the Soldiers' National Cemetery.

However, President Lincoln had another goal. He wanted to reassure a wounded republic that the North would prevail. The president's speech, although short, proved to be both moving and inspiring.

Today, Lincoln's Gettysburg Address is remembered as one of the most important speeches in American history.

Glossary

assassinate - to murder a very important person, usually for political reasons.

banter - good-humored, teasing conversation.

bunting - decoration made of fabric.

canteen - a container for liquid, usually water.

compliment - a feeling or expression of praise or liking for something.

comprehend - the act of understanding something.

Confederacy - the country formed by the states of South Carolina, Georgia, Florida, Alabama, Louisiana, Mississippi, Texas, Virginia, Tennessee, Arkansas, and North Carolina when they left the Union between 1860 and 1861. The people were called Confederates.

conscience - the sense that one's actions, intentions, or character have moral goodness.

consecrate - to set apart or declare as holy.

convenience - a suitable time.

debate - to argue publicly about a question or a topic.

dedication - an act of setting aside an object or a place for a certain purpose.

detonate - to set off or explode.

detour - taking a different way to get somewhere.

distraction - anything that causes a person to lose focus or direction.

drastically - with extreme action.

eerie - strange or creepy.

Emancipation Proclamation - a famous paper written by President Abraham Lincoln in 1863. It says all slaves are free.

enthral - to fascinate.

generation - a group that is living at the same time and is about the same age.

hearth - the floor of a fireplace.

hospitality - having a welcoming and pleasant environment.

lunge - a sudden rush forward or reach.

memento - something that reminds a person of a place or an event.

procession - a group of people moving in an orderly way, often for some type of a ceremony.

rededication - the act of holding an event again to open something, such as a new building or park.

reverence - a feeling of awe or respect.

rural - relating to the country or farmland.

sacrifice - something given up or lost for the sake of something else.

secede - to withdraw from an association or organization.

silhouette - the outline of a figure or profile.

sinister - looking dangerous or evil.

solemn - serious.

spectator - a person who is watching an event take place.

transpire - something that happens.

Union - the states that remained in the United States during the Civil War.

urgency - the state of needing to do something quickly.

veteran - a person who has served in the military.

waistcoat - a vest.

wary - cautious and on one's guard.

About the Author

Maximilian P. Mouse, Time Traveler was created by Philip M. Horender. Horender resides in upstate New York with his wife, Erin, and their dog, MoJo.

Horender earned his Bachelor of Arts in History with a minor in education from St. Lawrence University. He later obtained his Masters in Science in Education from the University at Albany, the State University of New York.

He currently teaches high school history, coaches swimming, and advises his school's history club. When he is not writing, Horender enjoys biking, kayaking, and hiking with Erin and MoJo.